THE NIGHT BEFORE
PRESCHOOL

To the Billy bears and Boing Boing rabbits that are best buddies to kids heading off to school–N.W.

To Sean, who is going to have a lot of fun in preschool!—A.W.

GROSSET & DUNLAP
Published by the Penguin Group
Penguin Group (USA) Inc., 375 Hudson Street, New York, New York 10014, USA
Penguin Group (Canada), 90 Eglinton Avenue East, Suite 700, Toronto,
Ontario M4P 2Y3, Canada (a division of Pearson Penguin Canada Inc.)
Penguin Books Ltd., 80 Strand, London WC2R 0RL, England
Penguin Group Ireland, 25 St. Stephen's Green, Dublin 2, Ireland
(a division of Penguin Books Ltd.)
Penguin Group (Australia), 250 Camberwell Road, Camberwell, Victoria 3124, Australia
(a division of Pearson Australia Group Pty. Ltd.)
Penguin Books India Pvt. Ltd., 11 Community Centre, Panchsheel Park, New Delhi—110 017, India
Penguin Group (NZ), 67 Apollo Drive, Rosedale, Auckland 0632, New Zealand
(a division of Pearson New Zealand Ltd.)
Penguin Books (South Africa) (Pty.) Ltd., 24 Sturdee Avenue,
Rosebank, Johannesburg 2196, South Africa

Penguin Books Ltd., Registered Offices: 80 Strand, London WC2R 0RL, England

Text copyright © 2011 by Natasha Wing. Illustrations copyright © 2011 by Penguin Group (USA) Inc.
All rights reserved. Published by Grosset & Dunlap, a division of Penguin Young Readers Group,
345 Hudson Street, New York, New York 10014. GROSSET & DUNLAP is a trademark of
Penguin Group (USA) Inc. Printed in the U.S.A.

Library of Congress Control Number: 2010022197

ISBN 978-0-448-45451-1

10

THE NIGHT BEFORE
PRESCHOOL

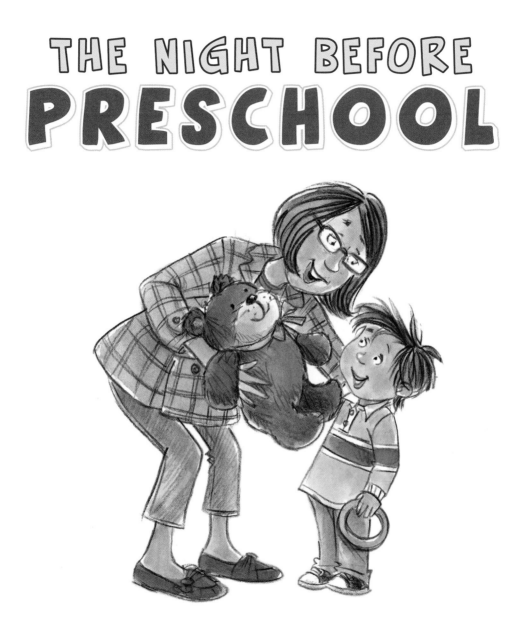

By Natasha Wing • Illustrated by Amy Wummer

Grosset & Dunlap
An Imprint of Penguin Group (USA) Inc.

'Twas the night before preschool,
alarm clocks were set.
All the children were cuddling
their favorite plush pet.

Monkeys and lions
and soft bunnies, too,
would be going to school
like big boys and girls do.

Parents set out clothes
and clean underwear.

Hoodies were hung
by the front door with care.

The children then nestled all warm in their beds,

while visions of playtime danced in their heads.

But one little boy
was still wide awake.
He worried about preschool
and the friends that he'd make.

His tummy hurt,
yet he didn't know why.
He hid behind Mommy.
He was feeling quite shy.

"Hi there, Billy!" said Justin.
He greeted each child by name.
"Gather 'round and we'll start
with a fun clapping game."

Kids sang songs and danced dances—they loved Circle Time!
Then everyone listened to stories and a Mother Goose rhyme.

They dressed up in clothes
from the big costume box.
"Look! I'm a pirate!"
"And I'm Goldilocks!"

But Billy just watched
other kids as they played.
In the corner by himself
was right where he stayed.

He drew a dinosaur
as tall as a tree.
He showed it to Justin.
"That's great! Is it for me?"

Then the children picked up their crayons and toys
and took a trip to the bathroom—
one for girls,
one for boys.

"Let's break for snacks!" said Justin. But Billy pushed his aside.

Then off the class marched for playtime outside.

There were tricycles to ride in a big loop-the-loop,
a garden to tend, and sandpiles to scoop.

After hanging up jackets and wiping off shoes,
they gathered their buddies for a quiet-time snooze.

The kids lay on their mats; soon there wasn't a peep—
all were quiet except Billy who could not fall asleep.

"I can't take a nap
without my teddy, Jerome.
But he's not here," wailed Billy.
"I left him at home."

When what to his watering eyes should appear,
but a soft, fuzzy rabbit with a bow on its ear.

"It's okay," a little girl said. "Here, take my bunny."

And suddenly Billy's tummy
stopped feeling so funny.

"Thanks," whispered Billy,
snuggling up for a nap.

And just like that—
he was asleep in a snap!

After naptime was over,
he played with Charlene.
"I'll be the blue rings!" said Billy.
"And I'll be the green!"

When out in the hallway,
there arose such a clatter.

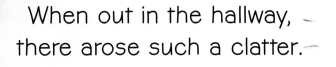

Kids sprang to the door
to see what was the matter.

Parents rushed in wanting hugs and kisses.

Billy's mom brought Jerome and asked, "Did you miss us?"

"See you tomorrow,"
said Justin.
Wow! The first day
was done.

"I'll be back," Billy shouted. "Preschool is fun!"